SAVE THE OCEAN

WRITTEN AND ILLUSTRATED BY

Bethany Stahl

Published in Knoxville, TN

ISBN:
978-1-7323951-2-1 Paperback
978-1-951987-17-6 Hardcover

Somewhere in the ocean, surrounded by a sea of beautiful creatures, lives Kaleisha, a brilliant young mermaid.

Save the Ocean
Save the Arctic
Save the Bees
Save the Land
Save the Scraps
Save the Sharks
Save the Butterflies
Save the Sky
Save the Air
Save the Reef
More coming soon...

One day, a sea turtle named Agwe swam by Kaleisha's coral home. He was on his way to find a delicious meal of jellyfish; Agwe's favorite!

"Can I come with you today?" Kaleisha asked. She hoped she could see more of the reef with her good friend who was almost one hundred years old!

"Of course you can, Kaleisha! Grab on to my shell and let's go!" Agwe laughed as he swam forward with the current of the ocean.

"Oh look! I see some jellies over there!" Kaleisha exclaimed as she pointed to a group of jellyfish.

With a big smile, Agwe bolted towards the jellies. He ate so many, like they were candy.

Kaleisha noticed something was wrong with Agwe. He was choking on a jellyfish! Kaleisha rushed to grab the jelly and pull it out of Agwe's mouth.

"This isn't a jelly!" Kaleisha frowned.

She turned to the other jellyfish, and realized that most of them weren't jellyfish at all! They were plastic bags that had washed into the ocean. But they looked exactly like jellyfish.

"This has been happening more and more," Agwe said sadly, still feeling hungry. "There have been more bags and less food for me to find."

"Oh, Agwe, this is terrible! How do we clean up our oceans?" Kaleisha asked her friends.

"REDUCE.
REUSE.
RECYCLE."

"Those are great ideas! We can help each other recycle, and teach everyone to use reusable bags instead of plastic. Then, turtles like Agwe won't accidentally eat trash anymore," Kaleisha explained.

"Recycling plastic containers and using reusable straws will help sea creatures. Together, we can reduce the trash in our ocean, so we can all enjoy a cleaner Earth!" Kaleisha said.

Everyone worked together to recycle their trash and protect the ocean. Soon, the ocean became clean again!

"I love eating jellies!" Agwe said.

"And I love you," Kaleisha replied, happy that she could help keep Agwe safe.

WATCH THE ANIMATED
AUDIOBOOK AT

BETHANYSTAHL.COM/TEACHERS

HOW TO REDUCE, REUSE AND RECYCLE!

1) Try using different containers than plastic. You can REDUCE how much plastic you use.

2) REUSE plastic and make it have a new use! Plastic containers are great for filling with rain to water your plants with!

3) Make a special recycling bin where your plastic can go. When you RECYCLE plastic the recycling center will make it into something new!

SEARCH & FIND!

Can you find a shark lurking on the outside of the reef in the book?

How many hidden starfish can you find?

Can you count how many jellyfish there were?

How many plastic bags did Agwe think were jellyfish?

Bethany's Sketchbook

OCEAN FACTS

There are only SEVEN different types of sea turtles!

The different types are green, hawksbill, Kemp's ridley, leatherback, loggerhead, olive ridley, and the flatback! Agwe is a green sea turtle.

Coral Reefs are home to more than 25% of all ocean life and only take up less than 1% of the entire ocean floor!

It takes the plastic bags, that turtles like Agwe accidentally eat, 10-1000 years to decompose. That is about ten human lifetimes, which means a bag you use could still be in the ocean when you have a great great great great great great great grandchild!

If we all work together, we can make a change!

More from the

Save the Earth® series!

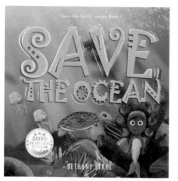

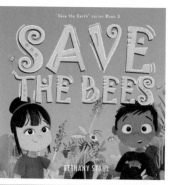

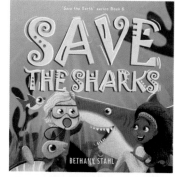

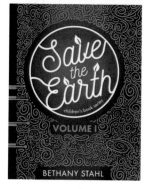

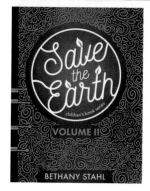

More titles coming soon!

ABOUT THE AUTHOR

Bethany Stahl is an award-winning, bestselling author of children's fiction. She dedicates her free time to helping green spaces in her community and giving back by regularly donating books to Little Free Libraries.

"Save the Ocean" is the first book in the "Save the Earth" series. Bethany grew up on the beach and started a branch of Jane Goodall's' "Roots and Shoots" program in Pinellas County High Schools while earning her Bachelor of Science in Biology degree. The group was dedicated to regrowing native plants' population and bringing awareness to saving sea turtles and other local endangered animals. Jane Goodall recognized Bethany's group efforts, and she received a Certificate of Recognition. Bethany has also dedicated over 1,000 hours of volunteering to protect and save our wildlife!

Bethany planting native plants!

Bethany rescuing a baby manatee!

Bethany diving with a sea turtle & supporting conservation efforts!

Bethany meeting Jane Goodall!

Made in the USA
Middletown, DE
18 April 2023